JAKE VS. THE SUPERNATURAL: GHOST NINJAS

PETER PATRICK

WILLIAM THOMAS

Jake vs. The Supernatural: Ghost Ninjas

Peter Patrick, William Thomas

Copyright © 2023

1st edition.

Also By Peter Patrick and William Thomas

Agent Time Spy Series:

Agent Time Spy 1
Agent Time Spy 2
Agent Time Spy 3
Agent Time Spy 4

*****

Middle School Super Spy:

Middle School Super Spy
Middle School Super Spy 2: Attack of the Ninjas!
Middle School Super Spy 3: A Giant Problem!
Middle School Super Spy 4: Space!
Middle School Super Spy 5: Evil Attack!
Middle School Super Spy 6: Daylight Robbery!
Middle School Super Spy 7: Pirates!
Middle School Super Spy 8: Missions!

*****

Diary of a Ninja Spy:

JAKE VS. THE SUPERNATURAL: GHOST NINJAS

BOOK 1

PETER PATRICK

WILLIAM THOMAS

CHAPTER 1

I wish I was awesome.

It would be awesome to be awesome. It would be so awesome to walk around all day in my awesomeness and act awesome while thinking awesome thoughts and doing awesome things.

Except I'm not awesome. Nope. Not even close. I'm about as far from awesome as Jupiter is from Earth, which is around 365 million miles. So, yep. That's a lot.

My name is Jake Matthews and I'm just a regular twelve-year-old kid doing regular things on regular days. Just regular old things like pulling chewing gum from my hair.

And my face. And my shirt.

I don't even know how I got so much chewing gum on me. I was sitting in the school cafeteria during lunch, minding my own business and chewing some gum when I coughed, sneezed, and burped all at once.

The chewing gum incident has only added to my already crazy day.

This morning our science teacher, Miss Boom, taught us how to make invisible ink by mixing lemon juice and vinegar together. She also taught us how to expose invisible ink by holding the ink close to a light bulb. Armed with this knowledge, our class spent the morning looking at super old books and checking if there were any secret messages written in them. The first message we found said, 'I was going to tell a joke about pizza, but it was too cheesy.' Strange thing to write, but hey, you can write what you want if you have invisible ink.

The second message we found was in a book that was two hundred years old. It said, 'You must stop the spirits from getting the invisible ink.' Weird message, right? Miss Boom didn't know what it meant, but people from two hundred years ago were known to be a bit strange.

We do a lot of weird things at my school. This year, the school added a 'Rock Observation Class for Kids,' or 'R.O.C.K' for short. In R.O.C.K, we sit down and stare at large rocks and see if they grow. We've done five classes so far this year, and nothing has happened yet.

"Jake! We're over here." My friends, George and Indie, called out to me and waved me over to our usual table in the cafeteria near the window. I hurried over.

"Hey guys," I said as I slid into the empty seat across

next to my friends. "What's up?"

"It's a children's movie about an old guy who makes his house fly away," George said as he took a sip of his soda.

"No, not what's 'Up,' I mean, what's up, like how are you doing?"

"How are we doing what?" George looked at me. "And nice hair, Jake."

I shook my head as I yanked another piece of chewing gum from my hair. There's no doubt that George is the smartest guy I know, he gets straight As in every class, even R.O.C.K, but sometimes, he can also act like the dumbest guy in the world. Yesterday, he went to drink out of his water bottle but accidently grabbed the ketchup bottle and drank out of that instead. He took five large gulps before he realized his mistake.

"I'm not even going to ask how you got that much chewing gum in your hair, Jake," Indie, my other best friend, said. "Only you could do something like that."

Indie is the coolest of my friends. She's so cool

because she's amazing at everything she does. She's awesome at sailing, swimming, surfing, skating, skydiving, sliding, stretching, sprinting, spelling, sewing, singing, shopping, sleeping, and snacking. So super cool.

The coolest thing I've ever tried to do was organize a professional Hide and Seek tournament, but it was a complete failure. Good players were hard to find.

"Have you heard the rumors about the Ghost Ninjas?" George asked.

"Ghost Ninjas?" I questioned.

"Yeah. Ghosts who are also ninjas. Every one hundred years, they come out of hiding and search for the one thing that can destroy them. And do you know what else?"

"That no one knows what it smells like underwater?"

"No, Jake. Well, I mean, yes, but—"

"Or that every word started out as just a noise until one person convinced enough people that what they said was a real word?"

"Well, yes, but that isn't what I was saying." George

shook his head. "I was going to say that this year is exactly one hundred years since the last sighting of the Ghost Ninjas. They're due now."

"What do they want?"

"They've been roaming the lands for centuries, scaring people from country to country, ever since they were banned from their homeland in Japan. They've been searching for a particular chemical reaction, and they need to find the formula before anyone else does." George leaned in closer and lowered his voice. "They need to find the secret formula before it can be used against them."

"It's just rumors," Indie added. "Nobody has proof that the Ghost Ninjas even exist. It's just an old story to scare little kids away from dark places."

"It would be so awesome if that was true," I said. "Can you imagine if we discovered proof that the Ghost Ninjas were real? We'd be mega famous. If we could just get one video of them, we'd be the most famous people on the planet. How cool would that be?"

"No chance, Jake," Indie added. "The Ghost Ninjas wouldn't want to come to our town."

She was right. Nothing exciting ever happens around here.

"But enough about the Ghost Ninjas. We still have schoolwork to do." George took his math book out of his bag and placed it on the table. "Miss Take wants us to study the section on Pythagoras' theorem before tomorrow."

"I don't know much about Pythagoras and his triangles, but that math book looks really sad," I said.

"Why do you say that?"

"Because it has so many problems! Ha! Get it? Problems—math problems?"

George shook his head and didn't laugh. Indie rolled her eyes. Just as I was about to tell another awesome joke, the school bell rang.

Great. This afternoon I have sliding class. That's where we learn to slide along the floor on our stomach. It's easier when the ground is slippery, and I totally don't recommend taking the class over rocks. Currently, my record for a slide is the length of the hallway, but our teacher, Mr. Slipper, holds the school record. He slid down the hallway, around the corner, through the science class, down the next hallway, and out the door. His father, grandfather, great-grandfather, and great-great-grandfather were also school sliding champions.

After I got the last piece of chewing gum out of my hair, I walked out of the cafeteria toward the gym, with my friends following a step behind. We walked outside, taking the path to the gym that went past an old, abandoned part of the school.

As we crossed the football field, I noticed something strange. In the bushes to the left of the field, the shadows were moving.

"Guys," I said. "Do you see that?"

"The shadows are changing." Indie shivered. "What is it?"

"I don't know," George whispered, cowering behind my shoulder for a second. "And I don't want to know."

And then, the shadows were gone. Just like that. They disappeared into thin air.

"What do you think it was, Jake?" Indie asked.

"Ghost Ninjas," I said. "We need to find the ghosts and get a video of them. This is our chance to become mega famous."

CHAPTER 2

I couldn't stop thinking about the moving shadows.

It was all I could think about during sliding class. The shadows had been looking at me, staring at me, peering into my soul like they knew me. I could feel them watching me.

When the final bell of the day rang, I raced outside to see if I could see more of the moving shadows, but as soon as I stepped outside, I stopped. I should've walked out into the hot air. It was still summer, and the sun had been burning hot for weeks. The weather report had said that the heat was going to continue.

Except it didn't.

As soon as I stepped outside, I was freezing. The sky had become cloudy, the air was still, and the temperature had dropped dramatically. It felt like it was almost cold enough to snow.

"It was hot at lunch time. What happened to summer?" Indie asked as she came up beside me, her arms wrapped across her chest, trying to keep warm. "It's like the seasons changed within an hour."

"I don't know what happened," I replied. "But I think it's something to do with the shadows we saw."

I looked to the bushes and watched for any movements, but I couldn't see anything. Indie, George and I decided to ignore the bushes and started the walk home.

As soon as we were off school grounds, the weather started to warm up again. It was like the cold weather had only been focused on the school grounds. We all thought it, but we were too afraid to say anything to each other. We walked in silence for a minute before George nudged my elbow.

"Uh, guys," George said. "Do you feel like we're being followed?"

I stopped and looked behind us. There was nobody there, but I had felt it as well. It felt like someone was watching us.

George pointed toward the bushes near the edge of the school football field.

Indie studied the bushes for a few moments. "I can't see anything."

We were all spooked by the talk of the Ghost Ninjas that afternoon, not to mention the moving shadows, so we walked a little closer together for safety.

"They say the Ghost Ninjas have crazy superpowers," George whispered. "And they're really powerful. Ghost Ninjas are more powerful than any superhero that's ever been created."

Indie nodded. "I've heard they can do all kinds of stuff, like move things with their minds, and they can fight like mad."

"And there are stories that the Ghost Ninjas can beat people up with their ghost weapons. Crazy, right? The ghost weapons can actually hurt people. That can't be real, right?"

My friends looked at me expectantly, waiting for me to tell them they were just stories. Reassure them, maybe. I was quiet for a moment, trying to think of something clever or funny to say.

Before I could open my mouth, someone screamed from behind us.

The scream came from an abandoned building at the edge of the school grounds. The red-brick structure was a disused teaching building that had been empty for years. It was all boarded up. Vines were growing all over it and there was grass growing on the roof.

We turned around and saw a girl running toward us as fast as she could go. It was Millie, a girl from my sliding class. Her long brown hair flew behind her like a cape as she ran toward us with terror in her eyes.

"The ghosts are here!" she screamed as she approached us. "I've seen them! They're right behind me!"

This must be her idea of a joke. Right? Right?!

But Millie wasn't laughing. She sprinted past us and further down the street without stopping.

George, Indie and I all waited for something to follow her, but nothing else came.

"Now people are seeing ghosts at our school?" Indie asked, her voice shaking as she looked over her shoulder, her face crawling with fear. "Maybe the stories are true? Maybe there are Ghost Ninjas in our school?"

"I don't know if I believe all of this," George said, shaking his head. "Ghost stories are one thing, but Ghost Ninjas? They wouldn't be in our town, right?"

We stood at the edge of the school, staring back at the dark abandoned building.

"I think we should investigate these stories about the Ghost Ninjas. Tonight."

George and Indie stared at me like I was crazy.

"Don't you want to know if the stories are true?" I continued when they didn't respond.

"No." George shook his head. "Uh-uh. No way. Not even in the slightest. I don't want to know if the stories are true. I don't want to know if any supernatural stories are true."

"Me either," Indie said. "No way."

"Imagine if we were able to record them?" I replied. "Wouldn't it be awesome if we got a video of the Ghost Ninjas to prove that they exist? Think about how famous we could become. If we post the video onto social media, we'll become internet sensations. We could be the most famous Ghost Ninja hunters of all time. How awesome would that be?"

George nodded slightly, but Indie just raised her eyebrows at me. She had no interest in becoming famous, but George liked the idea.

"We'll meet back here tonight and search the abandoned building. Be ready for a crazy night," I said. "It's time to find out if the Ghost Ninjas are real."

CHAPTER 3

I spent the evening thinking about ghosts, and I started to feel sorry for them.

Those poor ghosts are flying around all night long with no stomach, unable to eat donuts. Or chocolate. Or chocolate-covered donuts with ice cream and sprinkles. I guess all they could eat is air. Air sandwiches, air dinners, and air desserts. Those poor, poor ghosts.

Indie and George were waiting for me outside the school at 8pm, just after the sun went down. With all the lights off at the school, the whole area was pitch black. Indie and I were dressed in black, but George was dressed in his bright red pajamas.

"Why are you wearing bright red?" I asked George.

"Because you said to be reddy."

"No, I said to 'be ready,' like ready for anything." I

shook my head. "Ready, not reddy like the color. Ready."

"Oh, ready," George said. "That makes more sense."

"What did you tell your parents?" I asked while I started to sneak along the side of the main school building, trying not to trip in the dark. I winced as a branch smacked me in the nose.

"I told my Dad I was walking Angel Fluffy-Bottom," Indie said, pointing to her dog. "My Dad was just glad he doesn't have to do it."

Angel Fluffy-Bottom was a small dog, with a black and tan coat that shone in the moonlight. Her ears were small and triangular, and her nose was pink. She had two brown eyes and was always full of energy, even when she was sleeping. She looked like a complete angel, but she had a very fluffy bottom, and not the furry type either. I'm talking smelly fluffs.

"And I told my parents that I was studying the effects that moonlight has on juggling trumpets," George added. "I don't think they believed me, but they were just happy I was leaving the house."

"Well, I told Mom that I was gathering food for my dessert sandwich," I said.

"Dessert sandwich?" Indie raised her eyebrows. "What even is a dessert sandwich?"

"You've never had a dessert sandwich? I have all sorts of dessert sandwiches. I have ice cream sandwiches, chocolate sandwiches, chocolate cake sandwiches—"

"A chocolate cake sandwich?" Indie asked. "Only you could eat that."

I love a chocolate cake sandwich. Even better is a chocolate cake hotdog, but that's another story for another day.

Through the darkness, we continued toward the school and the abandoned brick building at the back of the football field. It was an old brick building near the woods at the far end of the school. The building had weeds growing all over it, and some of the windows had been broken. There was no light inside, and it looked so dark that it could've been a black hole.

We stopped at the edge of the football field and

studied the abandoned building from afar.

"I searched for the building plans online, and I found the old building designs," George said. "There are five classrooms inside, connected by a long hallway, with a small staff room at the back of the building. The building hasn't been used for the last fifteen years, and there are plans to pull the whole thing down, but everyone is scared to go near it. They tried to demolish it once, but all the workers ran away from it. They say it's haunted."

All I really knew was that it looked totally spooky. If it wasn't full of ghosts, it would probably be full of zombies. Or monsters. Or anything super extra-scary, like math teachers. We snuck toward the building and a cloud covered the moon. The whole area became so pitch black that I could barely see my hand in front of my face.

"Let's go back," George whispered, and then he paused to think up an excuse. "It's getting late, and I need to learn how to dance the Charleston. It's our homework for geography class."

I didn't believe his excuse, so I shook my head and

kept walking toward the building. George could turn back if he wanted, but I needed video evidence of the Ghost Ninjas. If we could just get one video of the existence of Ghost Ninjas, we'd be super famous.

As we got close to the entrance of the old red-brick building, the air became extra cold again.

I stopped just outside the front entrance and took my cellphone out of my pocket, pressing the record button. I looked behind me and nodded to George and Indie. Indie took out her flashlight, still holding onto Angel Fluffy-Bottom. George looked too scared to even move.

Taking a deep breath, I pushed open the door to the abandoned building. It creaked loudly and a heap of dust blew up. Nothing moved.

Slowly, we tiptoed inside.

"Eww," Indie whispered, waving her hand in front of her face. "This place stinks."

She was right. The hallway smelled like a gym locker that had been left to fester for five years, with an added hint of musty old books and the faintest trace of smoke.

I held my nose as my eyes adjusted to the dark.

"This is so stupid. We shouldn't be here after dark. We're gonna get in trouble," George whispered. "Who even knows if those ninja ghosts are real? They might not even exist. Right now, we're just trespassing on school property."

"What's that?" Indie asked, pointing into the distance down the other end of the hallway, where something small was moving toward us. It looked like a shadow with eyes glowing in the dark; kind of like a cat but way bigger.

"Just a shadow," I said, trying to keep my voice calm. "I'm sure it's just a shadow."

George turned on his flashlight, and I held my cellphone up for video evidence. Indie walked behind us, with Angel Fluffy-Bottom behind her.

George's flashlight's beam illuminated only a few feet ahead of us, so we could barely see where we were going. It was so dark and dusty that even the flashlight wasn't much use. The shadow stopped moving as we approached.

"There's nothing here," I whispered.

To my left, there was a door labeled 'Science Room.' As I went to grab the door handle, I heard a loud clunking noise behind the door.

"What was that?" I whispered as my heart beat harder.

Nobody answered. They were too scared to even talk.

What was behind the door?

Was it a ghost? A gym teacher? Or something worse?

We stood frozen in place for a moment, and then George turned his flashlight toward the door.

"I don't think we should go in there," Indie whispered while Angel Fluffy-Bottom started to whimper at her feet. "There could be anything behind that door."

"But this is what we came here for," I said and reached for the door handle. "We need to go in there."

"Wait." Indie reached out and grabbed my wrist.

"Are you sure you want to do this? If we open that door, we could be in all sorts of danger."

I took a deep breath and thought about it for a moment. I was so nervous that my hands were shaking, but we'd never have the opportunity record a Ghost Ninja again. This was our chance. No matter how scary it was, we had to do it.

I held my cellphone up, ready to record. "I'll get the door and go in first. George, you follow me in with the flashlight."

It was too dark to see George's reaction, but I'm sure he wasn't nodding.

There was another loud clunk from inside the room. What was behind the door?

With my heart beating fast, I reached for the door handle. I twisted the metal handle, and it made a screeching sound, driving a shiver up my spine. I pushed the door open and a whole lot of dust flew up in the air.

Inside, the room was as dark as the hallway. It smelled like old socks, and I struggled not to vomit.

I stepped inside but couldn't see anything. The rising

dust was dulling the effects of George's flashlight. He moved the flashlight around the room, trying to look everywhere, but it was hard to see.

There were tables and chairs covered in dust, and on the tables were several strange machines; some looked like they might have been used as torture devices if they were still functional.

"This is way too creepy," Indie whispered as she shivered and pulled her jacket tightly around her shoulders. "And I've got a really bad feeling about this."

On the ground, next to one of the tables, there were test tubes and beakers... and they looked freshly used. It was if someone, or something, had been doing experiments in the room recently.

I stepped further into the room, holding my cellphone in front of me. My hand was shaking, and the video was nothing but darkness. My heart was racing.

And then, my cellphone battery died! No! Not now!

I should've charged it! Argh!

There was another noise. A creaking sound, followed by a deep moan.

George turned his flashlight to that direction. Something else moved in the shadows! What was it?

"Who's there?" Indie whispered. "Hello? Who's there?"

We had no idea what it could possibly be. But then we heard it again—there was a deep moan followed by a faint rustling sound coming from somewhere near the old chalkboard.

"Oh no," Indie said, clutching my arm tightly as we stared into the darkness.

The rustling grew louder until finally…

A Ghost Ninja came into view right in front of us!

I blinked and rubbed my eyes. He was terrifying.

He was a tall ghost dressed all in black, with glowing red eyes and long white hair flowing down his back. He stood there for a moment, staring at us with a look of anger on his face.

Then he floated toward us and spoke.

"You're mine." His creepy voice sent chills all through me. "I own you."

"Hey," I said to him. "You don't own me or my friends."

I started waving my arms around like I was doing kung-fu. I was making lots of movements, trying to scare him.

It worked. My awesome ninja movements frightened the ghost so much that he moved back into the darkness and then disappeared.

I grabbed George's flashlight and shone it all around the room, looking for any trace of the ghost, but there was none.

"What happened?" George whispered. "What was that?"

"We just saw our first Ghost Ninja." I said. "And I have a feeling it won't be our last…"

CHAPTER 4

"We have to get out of here," George said as he tugged on my shirt. "I don't want to see another one of those things."

"No way," I responded and took a step forward. "My cellphone died, and there could be a charger here for me to use!"

"Jake," George continued, "did you see that thing? I've never seen something so scary. We can't stay here. What if he comes back?"

"We need to find out if there's more of them and we need to get a video of them. We can't leave now— we're just getting started," I said as I looked for a charger in the room. "I need to get a video of a Ghost Ninja to prove that they exist. Nobody will believe us otherwise."

"I've never seen Angel Fluffy-Bottom so scared,"

Indie said as she pulled on her leash. Angel Fluffy-Bottom whimpered and hid behind Indie's leg. "She's usually so brave."

"We can't go yet," I pleaded with them. "This is our chance to be mega famous."

Indie grabbed my arm. "Jake, I have a really bad feeling about this. If Angel Fluffy-Bottom is this scared, I don't think we should go any further. George is right— we need to get out of here."

I was about to argue with her when I saw a shadow move to our left. Or at least, I tried to tell myself that it was just a shadow.

And then there was a low crying noise, like a little hum.

"Jake." George grabbed my shoulder and hid behind it. "We need to get out of here. Now."

"Not yet," I whispered. "I need to see if there are more of them."

The shadows were moving. I could sense something circling all around us. The hairs on my arms stood up and goosebumps covered my skin.

There was a scurrying sound, like something was scrambling across the ground.

"What was that?" Indie hid behind my other shoulder. Angel Fluffy-Bottom hid behind my leg.

"I'm not sure what's happening," I said. "But whatever it is, it's coming this way."

There was another scraping sound—this time closer than before—and then there was a loud bang. It sounded like someone had dropped something heavy on the ground nearby, like they'd just dropped an elephant on the floor.

We all jumped and looked at each other in fear.

There were even more Ghost Ninjas!

Right in front of us!

They were all wearing black masks and had ghost swords!

"Hands in the air!" a muscular Ghost Ninja said, pointing his finger at me. He must work out in the ghost gym lifting ghost weights, which I don't think would be very heavy. "Don't make any sudden moves!"

George dropped the flashlight, but it was still on. The light covered the left side of the room, and we could see the Ghost Ninjas clearly.

"Who are you?" I asked as I put my hands up in the air.

"I'm Shinobi, a Ghost Ninja," the ghost said with a low growl. "And now, because you've seen me, I need to take you prisoner! We have to take you away to our secret hideout." He paused and then started laughing, "You'll never escape from us!"

Uh-oh. That didn't sound good. Not good at all.

CHAPTER 5

Indie, George, Angel Fluffy-Bottom and I huddled together in the middle of the dark room. The room was so cold that we were shivering, and the smell of old socks seemed to be getting stronger.

More Ghost Ninjas appeared out of the shadows. There were at least ten of them, all with the same muscular frame, floating around the room, staring at us like we were all delicious chocolate cake sandwiches. George held onto my arm tightly. Indie was right next to me. Angel Fluffy-Bottom was at my feet.

"What are you going to do to us?" I asked.

"We're going to keep you hostage until you tell us where the formula is."

"The formula? What formula?"

"The formula that can end our existence," Shinobi

said as he floated closer to me. "We must have the entire formula, and we know that it's near this school."

"I have no idea what you're talking about. We don't know anything about any formula," I argued. "Now, that's sorted, it's time for you to let us go."

"No," Shinobi snarled. "We will hold you hostage until we find the formula. You're our slaves."

The Ghost Ninja started laughing. It was a crazy, evil laugh that sent chills down my spine. The other Ghost Ninjas started laughing as well. They didn't even say anything funny. Ghost Ninjas must have a terrible sense of humor.

"I'll distract them," I whispered to my friends while the Ghost Ninjas were busy chuckling. "And when they're distracted, we run."

"That's a terrible idea, Jake," Indie said. "How are you even going to distract them?"

"I have a plan."

"What is it?"

"I plan to be me."

"That's ridiculous," Indie said and looked at me, "but it's crazy enough that it just may work."

I turned back to the ghosts. It was my fault we were still here. I had to do something to save my friends. I couldn't let the Ghost Ninjas kidnap us.

I started waving my arms around like crazy, using all my best ultra-ninja moves, and the Ghost Ninja took a step back! Yes! It was working!

I flapped my arms harder, whirling them around as much as I could. The Ghost Ninjas moved back even further. Then it struck me—the ninjas weren't afraid of my moves; they were afraid of the wind I was creating!

The wind was pushing their ghost bodies backward!

"Run!" I yelled to my friends as the ninjas backed off. "Let's get out of here!"

We turned and ran, but it was so dark we didn't know where we were going. George ran into the wall, and Indie bumped into a table.

"Over here!" I yelled once I found the door. "It's the exit!"

We ran through the door of the room into the hallway, but the hallway was dark. I couldn't see anything!

"Which way?" Indie yelled.

"I'm don't know," I said, and then heard a noise behind me. I opened a door that led to another classroom. "Quick. In here. Get down and hide."

We stopped and hid in the darkness, hiding behind a table near the front of the room.

We crouched down with Angel Fluffy-Bottom. She was whimpering.

"It's okay," Indie whispered to her dog. "They don't know where we are. We just need to stay quiet."

Angel Fluffy-Bottom barked in response. I cringed and held my breath.

We heard shuffling noises again. They were close.

"Keep quiet," I whispered.

I looked over my shoulder. One of the windows was open. It was our way out!

"Let's go," I whispered as I pointed toward the exit. "It's not far."

We crawled out from behind the table, but no!

Five skinny Ghost Ninjas floated in front of us!

The skinny Ghost Ninjas had their swords in their hands, ready to attack us. Then they started laughing again. Why were they laughing? This wasn't funny at all! They have such a bad sense of humor!

One of the Ghost Ninjas slashed at Indie with his sword, but Indie ducked out of the way.

Then they swung at me!

I dodged the sword and dove to the side. I grabbed a large piece of cardboard off the table and flapped it around. The Ghost Ninja was pushed back by the wind, but then he came back again and lunged at me with his sword!

I dodged out of the way just in time again. The Ghost Ninjas circled around us in the dark, their swords raised high!

No! We were trapped!

Then Angel Fluffy-Bottom jumped out of the shadows and started barking.

"A dog!" one of the Ghost Ninjas shouted. "Just what we need!"

The Ghost Ninjas lunged at Angel Fluffy-Bottom, wrapping their ghost arms around her.

"No!" Indie shouted. She dove for the leash, but it was too late—the Ghost Ninjas had dragged Angel Fluffy-Bottom into the shadows!

"Aha!" George yelled triumphantly as he came out from behind the desk, waving his shirt around his head.

The remaining Ghost Ninjas were blown backward by the gusts of air from his spinning shirt!

"Take that!" George yelled, spinning his shirt around and around. "Get out of here!"

The skinny Ghost Ninjas weren't strong enough to beat the wind. They disappeared into the shadows!

George and I high fived and jumped into the air as we let out a little shriek of victory.

"Angel Fluffy-Bottom!" Indie yelled out as she reached for the flashlight on the ground. "My Angel!"

She picked the flashlight up and ran back into the old science room, looking for Angel Fluffy-Bottom.

"Help!" Indie cried as she ran around the room. "They've taken Angel Fluffy-Bottom!"

George and I ran into the room after her, but we couldn't see anything!

We looked everywhere but there was nothing. There was no sign of the Ghost Ninjas, no sign of any ghost sandwiches, and no sign of Indie's dog.

Angel Fluffy-Bottom had been dog-napped.

CHAPTER 6

Mom and Dad were waiting for me at the front door of my house. That wasn't a good sign.

"Jake, where have you been?" Dad demanded when I stepped through the door. "You promised you'd be back hours ago. It's 9:55pm. You should've called us. We were about to send out a search party looking for you."

"Sorry, Dad," I said, walking inside with my head down. "My cellphone died."

"That's no excuse."

"I'm tired," I said, hanging my head. "Can you please tell me what my punishment is in the morning?"

Mom opened her mouth like she was about to say, 'No way,' but then her face softened, and she looked sorry for me. "Go to bed. Sleep. And your punishment is to scrub the garage down on the weekend."

"Yes, Mom," I said and went to my room.

I fell onto my bed, but I couldn't sleep right away. All I could think about were the Ghost Ninjas and poor Angel Fluffy-Bottom.

Indie, George and I had searched for Indie's dog all through the abandoned building for an hour, but we couldn't find her, nor could we find any more Ghost Ninjas. They had completely disappeared. It was like they never existed.

Indie was shattered. After an hour of searching, George and I walked her home. Indie cried the entire way. We tried to reassure her that we would find Angel Fluffy-Bottom in the morning when it was daylight, but I wasn't so sure.

Angel Fluffy-Bottom had just disappeared. She was taken into the shadows by the Ghost Ninjas and completely vanished. I'd never seen anything like it. She was just… gone.

After hours of stressing out, I finally got to sleep, only to have a nightmare. I was standing in the middle of an empty warehouse and there were Ghost Ninjas everywhere. They were eating green bananas and yellow broccoli, and talking about how much they loved scaring people. I asked the Ghost Ninjas for a marshmallow, and they handed me a giant one. The marshmallow was very chewy, and I couldn't eat it. Then, I turned into a tiny kangaroo and told the Ghost Ninjas to stop harassing Angel Fluffy-Bottom, but the Ghost Ninjas just laughed at me. They called me 'Mr. Tiny Kangaroo Head.' "No!" I yelled in my dream. "My name is not Mr. Tiny Kangaroo Head!"

There was a loud bang as Mom came into my room and shook me awake. She turned on the lights and handed me a glass of water before sitting down on the edge of my bed.

"You had a bad dream, Jake." She rested a hand on my shoulder. "Someone was calling you Mr. Tiny Kangaroo Head again."

"It was nothing." I shook my head. "Just a dumb dream where I thought I was eating a marshmallow."

I looked down at my pillow. It had bite marks in it. Oops.

"What else was the dream about?" Mom asked.

"It was a nightmare about ghosts."

There was a look of fear on Mom's face as soon as I said the word 'ghosts.' "You need to be careful, Jake. You're twelve now."

"Careful of what?" I asked, sitting up.

"Of —" She started to speak and then stopped herself again with a heavy sigh. "Never mind. You need to be careful not to be late for school. It's time to get up."

*****

I saw Indie as I approached the entrance of our school. I could see that she'd been crying most of the night. She explained that when she went home, she told her father that Angel Fluffy-Bottom had run off into the abandoned building at the school.

"He went out and searched for him for hours," she said. "He was out all-night. He only just got back as I was leaving for school."

"Did he find Angel Fluffy-Bottom?" I asked.

Indie shook her head, holding back the tears. "Dad spent all night looking for her but couldn't find a trace. Not even a trace. She just completely vanished."

"What did you tell him?"

"I told him that Angel Fluffy-Bottom ran off because she was scared of the dark."

"You didn't tell him about the ghosts?"

"I couldn't. It's a crazy story and we didn't get any evidence, remember?" She raised her eyebrows. "Did you tell your mom or dad about the Ghost Ninjas?"

"No way." I shook my head. "They wouldn't have believed me either. And what were we supposed to say—last night we went hunting for Ghost Ninjas but didn't get any video footage because my phone was dead. I mean, it sounds ridiculous. I'm starting to doubt it myself."

"But it did happen." Indie was firm. "I saw them with my own eyes. We all did."

Without evidence, we knew that if we told anyone else what happened—especially the grown-ups—they wouldn't believe us. Everyone would question why we didn't have video footage of the ghosts.

George approached us. He also looked extra tired.

"I didn't sleep at all last night. I kept having nightmares about the Ghost Ninjas," he explained. "And I'm so worried about Angel Fluffy-Bottom."

"Me too," Indie said.

"Me three," I agreed. I tried to tell a joke to cheer everyone up. "What do you call a magic dog? A Labracadabrador."

Nobody laughed. We were all too sad to laugh.

"This was all my fault," I continued. "I suggested we go to the school, and I said that we should stay even after we saw the ghosts. I'm sorry that I dared you two to come along."

"No way," George said. "We all went there together.

We're all responsible."

"Angel Fluffy-Bottom is a smart dog," Indie added. "We don't even know if the Ghost Ninjas kept her. Maybe she just ran away."

"What if they're hurting Angel Fluffy-Bottom?" I asked quietly. My eyes started to fill with tears at the thought of poor little Angel Fluffy-Bottom being hurt by the Ghost Ninjas. "Or turning her into one of them in their secret lair?"

"Like a ghost dog?" George questioned.

"We have to go back there and rescue her," I said. "We can't leave her there alone."

"No," George said. "We should tell our parents the whole truth first."

Indie and I looked at each other. It sounded stupid, but he was right. We should at least try to explain it to our parents.

It was time to tell the truth.

CHAPTER 7

After school, I walked home with Indie and George. We barely said a word to each other.

We agreed that we would present a united front to each of our parents. We went to George's house first and explained the situation to his mother and father. They were scientists and only believed what they could prove. We told them about the haunted building, about the ghosts, and about their attack on us. They didn't believe a single word we said. They thought it was the dumbest thing they'd ever heard, and it must've been a prank. We pleaded with them to believe us, but they told us to get out of the house.

We went to Indie's house next. Her parents didn't believe us either. Her Dad said we were making it up to cover up our mistake of losing Angel Fluffy-Bottom. He was still upset about losing the family dog.

We went back to my house next.

My Dad was at work, so we talked to my mom. We sat in the kitchen, and we explained everything. We explained that I'd wanted to be famous by taking a photo of a Ghost Ninja, but instead, we'd been attacked by the ghosts, and it had caused us to lose Angel Fluffy-Bottom. Surprisingly, she listened to everything we had to say, and she seemed to believe us.

Then I asked for her help, but she shook her head. "I'm sorry, Jake, but I can't help, even if I wanted to."

"Why not?"

"Ghosts can only be seen by children. Adults can't see them."

I stared at her in disbelief as I sat up straight. "What?"

She nodded. "You know how adults have a hard time seeing things that aren't there? It's because we lose our ability to see the supernatural." She paused for a moment and then sighed. "I used to be able to see things like ghosts as well. So did your dad. Your great, great grandfather wrote in a journal that he saw a Ghost Ninja once, exactly one hundred years ago."

"So, you believe in ghosts?" Indie questioned.

"Yes, I've seen ghosts before with my own eyes. But be warned—once someone turns fifteen, they can't see ghosts anymore. That's it. It's over. You can't see the supernatural world after you turn fifteen."

"Aren't you supposed to tell me that ghosts aren't real?" I took in a deep breath. Up until that moment I was still holding out hope that this was all some big prank. "Aren't you supposed to tell me that I'm just making this up, and that I have an overactive imagination?"

"Jake, now that you're twelve, it means you're the peak supernatural viewing age," Mom continued. "This is the age where you'll start to see all sorts of supernatural things. From now until you turn fifteen, you'll see a lot of supernatural things everywhere."

"Why fifteen?"

"It's the age when people start to believe less of what they see, and more of what they're told. We lose the magic that's inside us." Mom rested a hand on my shoulder. "Adults can't see the ghosts, but the ghosts can still cause havoc in our lives. I know they're around, but I can't see them anymore."

"What do we do then?" Indie asked. "How do we save Angel Fluffy-Bottom?"

My Mom looked at the three of us and said, "If you're the only people that can see the Ghost Ninjas, then you're the only people that can save her. But be careful. Be very, very careful. Ghosts can cause all sorts of damage to you. All those stories that you've heard about the Ghost Ninjas, all the stories about them hurting people in search of the formula, are true. They've been searching for that formula for centuries."

Indie, George and I were too shocked to respond. We sat in the kitchen with our mouths hanging open while Mom made us something to eat. I didn't even react when Mom placed a chocolate cake sandwich in front of me.

"Just be careful," Mom said. She gave me a kiss on the forehead, and then left the room.

I looked across at Indie and then at George. "Ghosts are real. Adults can't see them, so that explains why your dad couldn't find any evidence of the Ghost Ninjas when he went to the abandoned building."

I took in a deep breath and climbed up on the kitchen bench.

I stood up straight, clenched my fist, held it up next to my face, and looked to the distance. "Our parents can't help us rescue Angel Fluffy-Bottom. We're the only people who can stop the Ghost Ninjas. It's time to ghost those ninjas."

"Why are you on the bench?" Indie asked.

"For dramatic effect."

She shook her head. "And what does 'ghost those ninjas' even mean?"

"It's a cool catchphrase," I said, and jumped off the bench. "How about this one—it's time to ninja those ghosts?"

"Nope. That just sounds silly."

"It's time to super those supernatural beings?"

"Uh-uh."

"It's time to dance on the souls of the ghosts?"

"You can't dance."

"Good point. It's time to… um… it's time to tickle the ninjas?"

"We don't need a catchphrase," Indie said. "But we do need a plan to save Angel Fluffy-Bottom."

"Right. A plan. Got it!" I said and climbed back on the kitchen bench. I made a mean face, clenched my fist again, looked off to the distance and said, "I'm going back to the haunted school building tonight."

George looked at me like I was crazy. "Jake, I'm looking at you like you're crazy because you are crazy. What if you go back there and the Ghost Ninjas attack you again?"

I thought about it for a minute.

"Hmmm, yes, yes. I see the problem with that plan."

George did have a point—maybe going back there wasn't such a good idea after all, but then again, it was our only choice.

"Okay, so we need a better plan," I said, clenching my other fist. Both fists were now in front of my face. I narrowed my eyes and said, "I'm going to go back to the haunted school building tonight and ask the Ghost

Ninjas super nicely for your dog back."

Indie raised her eyebrows. "You're just going to ask them? That's your best plan?"

"Yep."

"But what if they don't give you Angel Fluffy-Bottom?"

"They have to," I replied. "It's not like they can keep her forever."

"But what if they capture you as well?"

"Indie is right," George said. "What if they take you as well?"

"They're not going to take him," Indie said. "Because we're going with him."

"Are we?" George looked at Indie.

"Don't be so scared," Indie said to George. "We're a team and we need to do this together."

Indie climbed up on the kitchen bench. She struck a dramatic pose. We waited for George. He sighed, before he also climbed up on the kitchen bench. For extra-dramatic effect, we all clenched our fists, held them out in front of us, and stared off to the distance.

"We're a super team," I said in my deepest voice. "And it's time this super team saved Angel Fluffy-Bottom."

CHAPTER 8

After darkness fell, my friends and I ventured back to the abandoned school building.

We stood outside as a cold chill filled the night air. A strong smell of five-day-old pizza was coming from inside the building. There was a low-level hum in the distance. I was scared, and I could tell that Indie and George were scared as well. But as spooky as it seemed, as creepy as it was, we had no time to lose.

We needed to save Angel Fluffy-Bottom.

"At least we know the ghosts won't lie to us," I said as we looked at the abandoned building.

"Why not?" George asked.

"Because if they lie to us, we'll see right through them."

George didn't laugh at my awesome joke. He just

stared at me with a stern look on his face.

"But maybe we can offer them their favorite dessert in return for Angel Fluffy-Bottom?" I waited a moment, and when George didn't respond, I continued. "All ghosts love ice-scream."

Again, nobody laughed. They must've been too scared to laugh.

Indie grunted and led the way around the building. George and I followed her, crouching low and trying not to make any noise as we approached. We sneaked up to one of the broken windows in the old science room and peered inside.

"Over there," Indie whispered, pointing to the far corner of the room. "There's movement in the shadows."

I stepped up and peered inside the old science room. It was dark but I spotted five Ghost Ninjas floating around the room. They moved with an easy flowing motion and didn't even seem to notice us watching them from outside the window.

"They're definitely up to something," I said. "I

wonder what it is?"

"Shh," George said, grabbing my arm. "They're talking. Let's listen to them."

We ducked down and listened through one of the windows, eavesdropping on their conversation while they made plans for our demise.

"We need to get rid of those kids," one of the ghosts said. "They're the only ones who can see us. If they figure out what we're up to, we could all be in trouble. We need to stop those kids before they stop us."

"What do you suggest?" another ghost asked.

"It's simple," the first ghost said. "We just need to tie up all the kids in the town, and then we'll be free to do as we like. No adult will be able to stop us."

What a lame plan. At least they didn't laugh like crazy people at their own plan. Oh, wait.

"Hahahaha!" The ghosts laughed together. "Hahahaha!"

Crazy ghosts. They kept laughing for a whole minute straight. I don't even get what was so funny. Ghosts have the worst sense of humor.

I looked at Indie and said, "Why can't you laugh at my jokes like that?"

"Because they're not funny."

Ouch.

Just when I was about to tell Indie my very best joke, we heard a familiar sound—Angel Fluffy-Bottom's bark!

I looked back through the window to see if I could spot her—and I did!

She was being held in a cage in the far corner of the room. She looked like she was ok, but the metal cage was small and tight. I ducked back down behind the window, and Indie and George crouched next to me.

"That's Angel Fluffy-Bottom," George whispered. "What are we going to do?"

"I don't know," I said. "But whatever it is, we need to do it fast."

We stood back up and looked inside at the Ghost Ninjas. One of the Ghost Ninjas was holding a map and pointing at different parts of it. Another was holding a sword in one hand and a knife in the other. The third ghost was trying to lick his elbow. Ghosts are so weird.

"Shh," Indie said. "They're talking about my dog."

I leaned my ear closer to the window so I could hear them clearly. "This dog has been able to smell out the chemical reaction," one Ghost Ninja said. "We know dogs have super sensitive smell, and she has confirmed that the formula is somewhere in this school. This kidnapped dog has been very useful."

Another ghost said, "But before we focus on the formula, we should get rid of the kids before they cause us any more trouble. Those kids will be able to tell the police about us."

"And if the police find out about us, they'll try and stop us. But if we get rid of the police, then nobody can stop us! We need to capture the police, tie them up, and we need to do the same to those kids. Then we can focus on finding the formula."

"That's a good plan," the other ghosts agreed. "Hahaha!"

Seriously? Why were they laughing? Why couldn't

people laugh at my jokes like that?

"They're going to take over the police station," Indie whispered. "We have to warn the police."

"Not yet," I said. "We need to get Angel Fluffy-Bottom back first." I braced myself. "And we've got to ghost those ghosty ghosts!"

"Um, nope. Still not a good saying," Indie said and leaned closer. "But how are we supposed to stop them? They're Ghost Ninjas and we're just three kids with no weapons, fighting skills, or plan."

"Look!" George suddenly said, pointing through the window. "Angel Fluffy-Bottom is free."

Angel Fluffy-Bottom had managed to sneak out of the cage. She was free!

I needed to move. There was no time to waste. Reacting on instinct, I jumped through the window and ran toward Angel Fluffy-Bottom!

But one of the Ghost Ninjas saw me! No!

"Stop right there, little boy," the Ghost Ninja said. "You can't take our dog."

"She's not your dog!" I yelled as I grabbed Angel Fluffy-Bottom and tucked her under my arm. "And I'm taking her home!"

I looked back to the window, but a Ghost Ninja had blocked the exit. I looked across to the other side of the room and saw another open window. It was time to go!

I took off running toward the other window, pulling myself up to the ledge, still with Angel Fluffy-Bottom tucked under my arm.

I braced myself and launched into the air. I shot through the window, just missing a beam.

But then I hit something hard, and everything went black.

CHAPTER 9

When I woke up, I saw Indie and George were sitting next to me in the dark abandoned school science room. I was cold and it took me a few moments to figure out where I was.

The air was so chilly it felt like we were sitting in a freezer. And I should know. I once hid in a freezer during a hide and seek competition. I was in there for five hours, and when someone finally found me, my face was blue, my fingers were blue, and even my hair had turned blue.

"What happened?" I asked as I rubbed my eyes.

"You blacked out after you jumped out the window," Indie said. "You jumped straight into a tree branch and knocked yourself out. Before we could get to you, a Ghost Ninja came out after you, and dragged you back inside. George and I jumped in here to save you, but they grabbed us as well. We tried to blow them away by flapping our arms around, but there were too many of them."

"Why didn't you run away?" I asked.

"Because you're our friend, Jake," Indie said. "We weren't going to leave you behind. As soon as they picked you up, we jumped in here to save you, but then the Ghost Ninjas surrounded us as well."

"Where's Angel Fluffy-Bottom?" I asked, turning around before my eyes adjusted to the light and I saw that Angel Fluffy-Bottom was in Indie's arms. She was safe.

"Enough talk."

Uh oh. It was one of the Ghost Ninjas. He didn't look friendly. In fact, he looked totally unfriendly. I think it was the scowl on his face that made him look unfriendly. That, and he was pointing a sword at me.

"We have captured you."

"Let us go," I said, getting to my feet. George and Indie stood up as well. The three of us stood back-to-back in a triangle position as the ninjas floated around us. "We don't want to be your friends."

"We don't want to be your friends, either," the Ghost Ninja replied.

"Oh, good," I said and starting walking toward the open window. "We'll just leave then. No problem."

"No," the Ghost Ninja grunted. "You cannot trick us."

"But… you don't have any brains."

"What?"

"I can literally see straight through your head, and I can't see any brains."

"Ah, yeah. Ok. Sure." The Ghost Ninja scratched his head, and then looked at the other Ghost Ninjas. "I hadn't thought about that. Do we have brains?"

"Of course not," I said. "And you've never thought about it because you don't have a brain to think about it."

"We have ghost brains," another one said, but then he turned to the others. "Don't we?"

"Uh?" Another responded. "I don't know. All we ever do is what our leader tells us to do."

"Yeah," another Ghost Ninja agreed. "We just follow orders from our leader."

The Ghost Ninjas all turned to each other and started discussing why they couldn't see each other's brains. They were distracted but still near the exit through the window.

"Don't worry," I said to my friends, patting my back pocket. "I have everything we need this time."

"Really?" Indie asked. "What do you have in there?"

"I have three fold-out fans," I said as I took out the fans. "It's enough to blow these brainless ghosts away."

"I don't know if I can fight these ghosts," George whispered as he pulled on my sleeve nervously. "They don't seem like nice ghosts."

"It's ok. Just pretend you're a skeleton."

"A skeleton? Why?"

"Because nothing gets under their skin," I said. Indie groaned. It was too dark to see if she also rolled her eyes.

But there was no more time for awesome jokes. It

was time to escape.

We started to tiptoe toward the window while the ghosts continued to discuss their brainless heads. We were halfway to the window when one of the Ghost Ninjas turned to look at what we were doing.

"Hey! Stop right there!" he yelled. He floated between us and the window, blocking our exit.

"What are we going to do?" Indie whispered to me, her voice rising in panic. "They're blocking the window."

"We have to make a break for the door and then into the hallway," I said. "I'll try to hold them off with my fan, and you and George open the door and lead the way through the hallway to the building exit."

Indie made a serious face and nodded. George made a scared face and shook.

"Ready," I said, with my fan held in my right hand. "Go!"

I started flapping the fold-out fan, pointing it toward the Ghost Ninjas, blowing them back with powerful forces of air.

Indie did a commando roll toward the door with Angel Fluffy-Bottom in her arms, and George followed. She pulled on the door, but it wouldn't budge. No! George reached out and helped Indie. With all their strength, they yanked the door open.

"We're through," Indie shouted. "Let's go, Jake."

I also did a commando roll toward the door. Then I did a pirouette, a grande jete, and then a tour en l'air. Man, those ballet lessons really paid off.

But despite my great ballet moves, the Ghost Ninjas followed me!

"We need to go fast!" I yelled, looking at Indie and George once we were in the hallway.

Together, we charged toward the hallway door, but two Ghost Ninjas appeared in front of the exit.

George held out his fan and started flapping it up and down! Yes! It was working! The ghosts were being blown back by the wind!

With an angry George charging forward and clearing the way, Indie, Angel Fluffy-Bottom and I followed through the exit. We sprinted through the door and onto the football field.

Once we were outside, we didn't stop running until we were off the school grounds. Near the fence, under a shining streetlight, we stopped to catch our breath.

Looking over my shoulder, I checked to see if the Ghost Ninjas had followed us.

I couldn't see anything. There was complete silence. It was as though there had never been another living soul in the school apart from us.

"They didn't follow us," I said. "We're safe… for now."

CHAPTER 10

Again, I didn't sleep.

I stayed up all night thinking about the Ghost Ninjas and their brainless heads. They were so scary and intimidating. I guess any ghost would be scary, but Ghosts Ninjas must be some of the scariest ghosts ever.

Except maybe ghost dentists. Or maybe ghost clowns would be the worst. Can you imagine it? Imagine looking out the window in the middle of the night and seeing ghost clowns carrying ghost balloons while riding ghost bicycles. That would be totally scary.

After not sleeping a wink, I met my friends before school, and we decided to go to the police station. We needed to warn them about the Ghost Ninjas. The Ghost Ninjas had a plan to take control of the police station and then take over the entire city, all in search of the mysterious chemical formula.

Confidently, we walked into the police station near the school. It was only a small police station with one door, one front desk, five police officers, and one baby hippopotamus. It was well-known that the police in our neighborhood didn't do much work. Crime was down, and they liked it that way.

I went to the counter and spoke to the first policeman, who sat behind a computer, barely acknowledging my existence.

"What do you want, kid?" he grunted after he finished his doughnut.

"Hi," I said. "Do you know what the policeman said to his large stomach?"

"What?"

"You're under a vest," I laughed. "Get it? A-vest. Arrest. I'm so funny."

The policeman didn't laugh. In fact, he looked quite grumpy. Maybe it wasn't such a good idea to open with a joke.

"Kid, I'm too busy for jokes. The biggest crime of the year has just occurred. We're calling it the 'Great Lemon

Heist.'" The policeman rubbed his hand over his bald head. "Someone has stolen all the lemons in our town, and we don't have any clues about who it was. Who would even want to steal all those lemons? We don't know who did it, and we don't know where the lemons are."

"What do you give to a sick lemon?" I continued with my jokes. "Lemon-aid!"

I laughed but the officer didn't. He didn't really like that joke either.

Our interaction only got worse from there. I tried to tell the police officer about the Ghost Ninjas and their plan, I tried to tell him about their search for the secret formula, and I tried to tell him about my favorite pizza sandwich, but he wouldn't listen to anything I said. He just kept grunting and groaning, before he told us to get out or he'd arrest us for trespassing.

Five minutes after we entered the police station, my friends and I were walking back out the front door, shaking our heads. The police didn't believe a single word of our story. It was clear they weren't going to help us stop the Ghost Ninjas.

Disappointed, my friends and I went back to school.

First, we learned about geography with Miss Align. She's not a very nice teacher.

Last week, Miss Align told us we were going on a class trip. The whole class was very excited, and she told us to stand in a line and close our eyes. We all stood up and waited. We didn't know at the time, but she was tying all our shoelaces together while we had our eyes closed. After a minute or so, she told us to keep our eyes closed and walk forward. With all our shoes tied together, we stepped forward. One by one, we all fell over. Miss Align laughed so hard she had tears running down her face. And we weren't very happy when she told us that was our class 'trip.' Yeah. She's not my favorite teacher.

After Miss Align shouted at us for an hour, we went to science class, but our teacher hadn't arrived yet. We were sitting in class for fifteen minutes before a substitute teacher came in. A chill in the air followed him.

"Hello students. My name is Mr. AJ Nin," the substitute teacher said. "Miss Boom has been tricked…

No. Not tricked. I mean, she's sick today."

Hmmm. Strange thing to say.

Mr. AJ Nin was dressed in a long coat, long trousers, and was wearing long gloves. He had a hat, a facemask, and he was wearing dark sunglasses, even though we were indoors. Not one piece of his skin was exposed. He also smelled like an old musty cupboard.

"Excuse me, sir." I put my hand up. "Are you wearing sunglasses because your pupils are so bright?"

I laughed, but Mr. AJ Nin didn't. He answered with one word, "No."

Ouch. Tough crowd.

"Students," Mr. AJ Nin continued, "if you have five bottles of lemon juice and one bottle of vinegar in one hand, and five cartons of baking soda and one carton of milk in the other, what do you have?"

"Big hands," I called out.

"No," Mr. AJ Nin responded. Clearly, he didn't have much of a sense of humor. "You have a chemical reaction. And we're going to talk about chemical reactions today to make invisible ink."

"But we did this last week with Miss Boom," George said. "Can't we do something else this week? We could learn all about the theories of quantum mechanics. I've heard that—"

"No," Mr. AJ Nin replied. "We must find the right formula to expose the invisible ink. That's our only focus."

"Groan," I said out loud and rolled my eyes. Why are teachers always making us repeat things? Like the times table. I already know that 0×0 is 0, and 1×1 is 1, and 'x' x 'x' is x-squared, so why do I have to do it five hundred more times?

Mr. AJ Nin ignored my groan and walked over to the science bench at the far-left hand side of the room, where there were half a dozen test tubes filled with different colored liquids. He picked up one of the formulas for invisible ink, the one filled with lemon juice, and held it over the other test tubes.

The whole class watched as he poured five tubes of different chemicals into another tube. He stood back in surprise at his own creation.

The mixture started bubbling and smoking, and smoke started to fill the room.

We all started coughing, and soon, there was so much smoke that we couldn't see anything. I was flapping my hand in front of my face, but I couldn't see a thing!

Behind the wall of smoke, I heard someone fall over and then there was a smash. Someone had broken some glass. With my arm covering my mouth, I ran to the side of the room and opened the windows, allowing the smoke to drift out.

When the smoke cleared, there was no sign of our substitute teacher, Mr. AJ Nin.

"Mr. AJ Nin?" I called out. "Hello?"

There was no response. I looked at the door to the classroom, but it was still closed. I looked under the tables—nothing. I looked in the cupboards—still nothing. I even looked in the drawers of the teacher's desk—nothing. Our substitute teacher had gone, vanished into thin air.

I got up and walked over to the bench, where there

was a broken test tube on the ground. There was a coat lying next to it. The tube of invisible ink was tipped on its side. The rest of the test tubes were still there, but there was no sign of Mr. AJ Nin.

I couldn't work it out.

We sat in class for another twenty-five minutes, waiting for him to return, but the bell rang, and we left to go to rock observation class. That class was a lot less eventful. Actually, nothing happened in that class at all.

And the rest of the day was uneventful until the end of our math class. The principal came into the room and asked about Mr. AJ Nin. Apparently, he had no record of Mr. AJ Nin on the school database. Very strange.

When I got home after school, I sat outside in the branches of my pet tree. I have a pet tree. His name is Treey-McTreeFace. Trees are the best pet you can have. You can talk to them, hug them, play tag with them (I always win), and as a bonus, Treey-McTreeFace even brings his own branches for playing fetch, although he doesn't fetch very well.

Sitting on one of the branches in my pet tree, I thought about lots of things. I thought about Mr. AJ Nin and what a strange teacher he had been. I thought about where Mr. AJ Nin had gone. I thought about his weird clothes. I wondered if a straw had one hole or two. And I wondered if clapping your hands was just high-fiving yourself.

Then it clicked. I reached for my cellphone and opened the group chat I had with George and Indie.

"GUYS!" I typed. "Mr. AJ Nin was no normal substitute teacher! Emergency meeting now at Indie's house. I will explain it all."

CHAPTER 11

I took a seat on the couch in Indie's living room.

I had raced over to Indie's house and my friends were waiting for me to tell them what I'd figured out. Indie was on the sofa brushing the hair on a Barbie doll, and George was playing a game on his cellphone. Both were apparently unfazed by the fact that our substitute teacher had disappeared into thin air earlier that day, or that super scary Ghost Ninjas were threatening the entire existence of our world.

"What do you call a line of Barbies?" I asked Indie. She shrugged and then I answered. "A barbie-queue!"

Indie groaned and shook her head. "What did you want to talk about, Jake?"

"While I was sitting with Treey-McTreeFace, I figured something out." I lowered my voice for dramatic effect. "I've found a way to stop the Ghost Ninjas from taking over our town."

George looked up from his cellphone. "Really?"

"The chemicals," I said, nodding. "We can use the same chemicals from science class that made Mr. AJ Nin disappear. The formula made him disappear, so it will make the Ghost Ninjas disappear."

"What makes you think it would work on the Ghost Ninjas?"

"Because I've figured it out—Mr. AJ Nin wasn't a human teacher."

"What are you even talking about?"

"Mr. AJ Nin was a Ghost Ninja dressed as a teacher!"

"What?"

"Think about it—the sunglasses, the gloves, facemask, and the long coat. We couldn't see a single piece of his skin. He was hiding his skin because he was a ghost! And remember how the room went cold when he came inside? He was a Ghost Ninja in disguise!"

"I don't know about that," George said. "That seems a little crazy."

"And what about his name? Mr. AJ Nin. Think about it! Its ninja spelled backward."

George looked at Indie and raised his eyebrows. Indie just shrugged as if to say, 'what can you do?'

I reached into my backpack and produced the test tubes that I'd borrowed from school. "Mr. Ninja was trying to infiltrate the school and find the secret formula. I went back to school and grabbed some of the formula. This must be what the Ghost Ninjas are looking for."

"But why would the ninjas be searching for a formula that makes them disappear?"

"Because this is the only formula that can defeat them! Once they gather up all of this formula, then nothing can stop them."

"So, we have to stop the Ghost Ninjas finding more of this formula by using this formula against them?"

"Exactly!" I clapped my hands together. Or maybe I high-fived myself. "When Mr. Ninja was in science class earlier today, he used this mix of chemicals."

"But he wasn't holding that test tube when he

disappeared," George added. "He was holding a different one. He was holding the one with lemon and vinegar, which is the one used to make invisible ink. That's what dropped on the floor."

"Don't be so crazy. This is absolutely the right formula."

"No, no, no." George shook his head. "That's not it. The chemicals you have in your hands are dangerous, Jake. You shouldn't play with those."

"Don't be silly. These chemicals are fine." I removed all the chemicals from my backpack and poured them together. The chemicals fizzed and bubbled in my hands as they mixed. The mixture was a fiery orange, like the sun setting over a tropical beach. "It won't hurt us, because we aren't ghosts."

At least, that's what I was counting on. I didn't really know for sure.

"I don't think it's the right one, Jake," George said as the bubbles started to become bigger. "You've got the wrong formula. The formula that we used today—"

"Nope," I said. "I'm sure this is the right one.

Absolutely. No doubt about it."

My heart was racing as I poured the mixture onto the ground and stepped back, waiting for it to make something disappear.

But instead, the bubbles grew bigger and bigger and bigger until...

BOOM!

Oops.

Wrong formula.

The blast was so big that it shook the entire building and blew us straight out the window of Indie's living room.

Outside, the three of us looked at each other in shock. Indie's face was pale, and George's eyes were wide.

"Hmmm." I put my finger on my chin as I sat on the grass. "Maybe you were right, George. Maybe it wasn't the right formula."

"Maybe?" Indie said. "What George was trying to say was that Mr. AJ Nin—"

"Mr. Ninja."

"Right. Mr. Ninja used a small drop of this formula to create the smoke, but the tube he was holding onto when he disappeared was the invisible ink formula. The formula used lemon juice and vinegar. That's the one we need to use."

"Oh. Right. Sure. That's a lot safer. Sorry about the windows, then." I stared back at the windows of Indie's house. "Let's make that formula instead."

Indie sighed, and led the way back into her house.

"Yes. Let's make the invisible ink formula before you blow us up again."

Our first attempt at the formula didn't work, but with Indie and George by my side, our second attempt would.

It was time to defeat the Ghost Ninjas.

CHAPTER 12

We had a plan. We had a team. Now, it was time to save the entire existence of the human existence.

Indie, George, and I spent the afternoon making more of the invisible ink formula. Indie only had one lemon left in her house, so we could only make three bottles of the formula. I ran home and checked my house for a lemon but there were none. Then I checked on my lemon tree and there were no lemons there either. I also checked the pineapple plantation nearby, but they didn't have any lemons either.

Still, we had enough lemons to make a spray bottle full of invisible ink formula each. That was enough, I told George, who was still super worried. I didn't really know if it was enough to stop the Ghost Ninjas, but I was willing to try and find out.

After nighttime fell, we gathered near the entrance to the school, each armed with a spray bottle of the formula. We were ready to attack the Ghost Ninjas and defend our town. These Ghost Ninjas picked the wrong kids to mess with.

Peeking out from behind a dumpster in the darkness of night, I watched the abandoned school building for any movement. It was creepy and deserted like usual, but this time I spotted a small light flickering on and off inside.

"Guys," I whispered. "This is the plan. We surprise the Ghost Ninjas and spray them with the formula. Once we hit them, they'll disappear. And once some of the Ghost Ninjas see how powerful we are, they'll surrender to us. After they've surrendered, we'll take some selfies with them." I tapped the fully charged cellphone in my pocket. "And then we'll be super, mega famous."

"Good plan," George said. "But what if the formula doesn't work? We don't even know if this makes them disappear."

"It will."

"But what if it doesn't?"

"Then we do what all clever people would do in that moment."

"What's that?"

"Run."

George and Indie nodded. We all took one last deep breath and then started to sneak toward the abandoned school building. My heart pounded in my chest as I led my friends closer to our destination, taking care not to make a sound. Every step echoed loudly in my ears—as if someone were tiptoeing right behind me, waiting for me to fall into their trap.

When we reached the entrance to the building, the front door was locked tight, which was strange because it hadn't been locked the previous nights. We had to find another way in.

"The window," Indie whispered.

Together, we crawled along the edge of the building until we reached the window to the old science room.

With a deep breath for courage and another for luck, I reached up onto my tippy-toes and pulled myself onto the window ledge until I could see inside. There was no movement. Not even the shadows were moving.

"It's not dangerous if we do it right," I whispered. "This is our chance."

"Let's just hope it works," Indie said nervously as she glanced around at our surroundings and shuddered slightly at how creepy the place was feeling.

"Maybe if we just leave them alone, they will get tired of being evil." George's voice shook as he spoke. "Maybe they really just want to be nice ghosts."

"George," I replied, "I don't think the Ghost Ninjas are just about to give up on their evil plans to take over the world."

"Yeah, maybe not," George said as he ran his fingers through his hair, which was sticking up in every possible direction.

Peering through the window again, I spotted two Ghost Ninjas at the far side of the room. They were playing a game of Rock, Paper, Scissors. I guess after hundreds of years of being ghosts, they still had to find a way to entertain themselves.

"We have to be quiet," I whispered. "There are two

Ghost Ninjas in the far corner of the room. We'll hit them first."

My friends nodded, and I helped Indie and George climb onto the window ledge. Indie quietly slid the window open, and then we snuck inside the dark and dusty classroom. We hid behind an old teacher's desk.

Five more Ghost Ninjas floated through the door and gathered in the middle of the room. They started discussing how they couldn't find Mr. AJ Nin, and that he'd completely disappeared.

"He must've found the formula," one ghost said.

"That means it's in the school somewhere," another added. "He spent the day dressed up as a teacher. He must've found it."

"It's go time," I whispered to Indie and George. "Let's do this."

"Let's do this," they replied together.

I took one more big breath and jumped out from behind the table with my spray bottle pointed at the Ghost Ninjas.

"Stop right there!" I yelled.

"Yeah!" Indie jumped out as well. "Stop right there!"

We waited a moment, but George didn't follow.

"George?" I whispered. "Are you still there?"

"Yes," he whimpered and stood up. His voice was shaky as he said, "Please, ghosts, may you cease where you are."

The Ghost Ninjas were all staring at us.

"What's in the spray bottles?" one asked.

"I have something that will make you evaporate," I said. "I've called it the 'Destroyer of Ghost Ninjas!'"

"Stupid name," one Ghost Ninja said and floated toward me.

Uh-oh.

I took a deep breath and held my spray bottle up. As soon as he got close enough, I sprayed and sprayed the formula at him. I hit five squirts of formula on his chest. He stared at me with a confused look on his face.

It took a moment, but he began to fade. He said,

"What is that?"

Before I could answer, the Ghost Ninja disappeared!

"Give me the formula!" The next Ghost Ninja lunged at me, but I was too quick for him. I dodged under his arm and sprayed him in the face.

He stumbled back, stunned by the formula. He disappeared as well.

Another lunged back at me. "I need more of that formula. I need all of it!"

Indie leaped forward and sprayed him. And the Ghost Ninja disappeared! It was working!

Another Ghost Ninja charged at us. This time, George used his spray to cover the ghost in the formula.

Yes! He disappeared as well!

But it was taking a lot of formula to cover the Ghost Ninjas and make them disappear. After only one ghost each, we were almost out of formula. Oh no!

Another Ghost Ninja charged at us, and then another. "We need that formula!" One of them yelled. "We need it!"

Together, we sprayed the ninjas charging at us.

"I'm out of formula!" I yelled when my spray bottle wouldn't spray any more.

"Me too!" George said.

"I'm out!" Indie added.

Oh no. This wasn't good.

Just as we were about to be defeated, the ninjas stopped charging at us. They all moved backward into the dark shadows.

And then, out of the shadows, one Ghost Ninja drifted forward slowly.

It was a tall man with a long black beard, dressed in a long black robe.

He must've been the leader.

He looked at me with his glowing red eyes and reached out to grab the spray bottle.

I was frozen in fear! I couldn't move!

"My name is Sensei Smiling Warrior," he said in a deep voice. "I'm the leader of the Ghost Ninjas. All Ghost Ninjas follow my orders. Now, give me that formula."

It was a strange name, because this guy looked like he hadn't smiled in hundreds of years.

Before Sensei Smiling Warrior could grab me with his long bony fingers, Indie yanked me out of the way and turned toward the window.

"Run!" Indie yelled. "Remember! That's the plan!"

"Right!" I snapped out of my fear and charged toward the window. "Let's go!"

George jumped out the window first, followed by Indie, and I was only a few steps behind.

We landed outside and sprinted across the oval, toward the other side of the school, before we stopped and looked back.

Sensei Smiling Warrior was hovering just outside the abandoned school building, staring at us from a distance. He still wasn't smiling.

After a few moments, he floated back inside the window and disappeared.

We were in the clear—for now.

CHAPTER 13

The next morning, we were all recovering at Indie's house after escaping from the school of doom with our lives. Indie made blueberry pancakes with whipped cream and syrup. She also offered to add her secret family recipe—pineapple, soda, and pea-flavored sauce—but I declined.

"I couldn't sleep last night. I kept thinking about the Ghost Ninjas," Indie said. "They made me so scared, so I forced myself to think about butterflies. I find butterflies so calming. I wish I could see a butterfly now."

I picked up the butter on the bench and threw it across the room.

"Jake!" Indie said. "Why did you do that?"

"Because you wanted to see butter fly. You said it calms you down."

"Not butter fly. A *butterfly*." Indie shook her head. "Like a beautiful little insect."

"Oh," I said and walked across the room to grab the butter. "Sorry."

Indie went back to eating the pancakes in silence. After breakfast, we sat on the front steps of Indie's house, worrying about how to stop the ninjas.

"Nobody can find any lemons," George said. "I asked my Mom to check at the shops, but all the shops had their lemons stolen this week."

"All the shops?" Indie asked.

"It's the 'Great Lemon Heist' that the police officer was talking about." George shook his head. "Even the lemons in people's homes have been stolen. Who steals lemons from homes?"

"Ghost Ninjas," I said. "They must've figured out that lemons were part of the formula and spent the week stealing all the lemons they could find. The other part of the formula was vinegar. Let's hope they don't figure that out."

"They really want that formula," Indie said, before

she threw a stick into the yard for Angel Fluffy-Bottom to fetch. "So, what do we do now?"

She looked at me like we were the experts in this situation.

"Well," I started slowly, "I don't think the Ghost Ninjas are going to just disappear now that they know the formula is here. They really want that formula, and I don't think they'll stop until they get it."

"We can't let them have it," Indie said as she took the stick back from Angel Fluffy-Bottom. "All I know is that we need more of that formula, and that means we need more lemons."

George nodded in agreement. "The Ghost Ninjas are going to be even more mad now. So, what do we do?"

We sat there in silence for a minute before Indie spoke up again. "What if we just went to the police station and told them the whole situation, and asked them to find some lemons?"

"But they didn't believe us last time," George added. "And they won't believe us this time either."

"The police are our best hope." Indie was firm. "And

we need to warn them about the Ghost Ninjas' plans to attack the police station."

CHAPTER 14

Although the police didn't believe us last time, we had to try again. The Ghost Ninjas were coming for them.

We walked into the police station, and there were five police officers near the front desk, still discussing the crime of the decade. They were so confused by the missing lemons. While waiting for their attention, we stood at the front desk and listened to them talk about the Great Lemon Heist. Apparently, even more lemons were stolen. The lemons were taken from shops, from houses, from trees, and even from the sloth racing stadium. Yep, we have a sloth racing stadium.

The police had taken the only lemons left in town and stored them under lock and key in one of the jail cells.

We waited for five minutes, listening to the stories of the Great Lemon Heist, before one of the officers turned to us. As soon as they spotted George, they all stopped and stared at him.

George was scratching himself all over because he decided to dress up as a ninja. "This ninja costume is really itchy," he whispered.

I went up to the front desk and spoke to the officer. "Hi. We need to talk to someone who can help us with something very important…"

"You again." The man looked down at me and sighed with a heavy, bored expression on his face. He looked at one of the other officers. "You guys can deal with these kids this time."

The biggest police officer turned toward me. He was a large man with a huge belly. I bet he could fit 155 donuts in that belly. Above his gigantic stomach, he had a badge that said Sergeant Doyle. He walked over to us and looked down at me.

"What do you kids want?" he asked. "And don't think we're going to fall for one of your stupid pranks. I won't believe in ghosts until I've seen them with my own eyes."

"We need your help," I said. "We need to talk to someone about some very serious problems that are happening right now."

Sergeant Doyle sighed. "I don't have time for this right now. Get to the point. And why is your friend dressed up as... some kind of ninja?"

"He's dressed that way because we need to show you what you're up against. We need your help—there are Ghost Ninjas in our town, and they're coming for you. They're behind the Great Lemon Heist and they're going to attack the police station later tonight." I pointed at George. "The Ghost Ninjas look just like this."

George performed some ninja moves, but even I'll admit that they weren't the best moves. In fact, it looked like he was dancing rather than attacking. The pirouette at the end really cemented that fact.

Sergeant Doyle looked like he was about to yell at me. "Look, kid, I don't know what kind of game you're playing, but there's no such thing as ghosts or ninja ghosts—and even if there were, they wouldn't try to take over our police station. Without photographic proof, we won't believe you. You need to go home and stop bothering people with your silly stories."

"Adults can't see them!" Indie stopped her foot. "Only kids can see the ghosts."

"So, they're invisible?"

"Only to adults," I explained. "But kids can see them."

"Right. And what are the made-up—sorry, invisible— ghosts going to do?"

"They're going to take over the police station and tie you up."

"Invisible ghosts are going to tie us up?" he chuckled. "Really? And how are they going to do that? With an invisible rope?"

Another officer appeared next to Sergeant Doyle. He wore a badge saying Officer Hardy. He was bald and much shorter than the other guy. He looked at us and said, "Another group of kids who want to tell us about their imaginary friends."

Before I could say anything, Indie jumped in. "This is real. You need to believe us. The Ghost Ninjas are going to attack the police station and tie you up. But if you don't believe us, I'll show you this." She pointed at George and said, "Okay, George. Show them what a Ghost Ninja can do."

George stared at her blankly for a second, then started jumping up and down on the spot like he was trying to fly.

After about fifteen seconds of this, he stopped and looked over at us. All the police officers were laughing and had tears rolling down their cheeks.

"I'm not laughing at you, I'm laughing with you," Officer Hardy said. "You're just…you're a very funny kid."

"I am not a kid," George said. "I'm twelve years old."

"You look like a kid," Officer Hardy said. "And if you really are twelve years old, then you would know that this whole thing sounds like an elaborate prank."

"But it's not a prank," I warned them. "It's real. The Ghost Ninjas are coming. You need to be prepared. And you need to give us all the remaining lemons."

"Go home kids." Sergeant Doyle's tone turned

grumpy. "I don't want to have to arrest a kid, but if you don't leave, I'll have to. I'll lock you up for trespassing."

"But—"

"Last warning, kid."

"Come on, George. Come on, Indie," I said, as we turned around. "We're going to have to save the city by ourselves."

CHAPTER 15

The first part of our plan had been a major loss.

A total fail, like the time George tried to talk to Amy Sting, a girl he liked. He had walked up to her with a bunch of flowers he picked from the school garden, but the flowers were home to a swarm of bees. When he gave the flowers to the girl, the bees sprung into life and poor Amy Sting was stung fifteen times. She didn't talk to him again after that.

Even with the failure of our first loss, I was still hoping that the second part of our plan could stop the Ghost Ninjas from taking over our city, and then the entire planet, and probably after that, the universe. Who knew how far these crazy ghosts could go?

Our major problem was the lemon shortage. We needed the lemons for the formula, but we had none left. We went door-to-door throughout our neighborhood, asking all our neighbors for lemons, but nobody had any.

Except for the ones at the police station, there was not a single lemon left in the entire town. We needed to find another way to make the formula.

"Maybe Miss Boom could help us," Indie suggested. "She's the smartest teacher I've ever met. Maybe she could tell us how to make a lemon substitute."

George and I agreed—we needed a substitute so we could make more of the formula.

George, Indie, and I walked five blocks to Miss Boom's house, which sat at the edge of a large park, which sat on the edge of a large cliff. It was a stupid place to have a park. Lots of frisbees, footballs, tennis balls, and drumkits had been lost over the edge of the cliff.

Miss Boom lived in a crazy-looking house. It was super skinny, but long, with only one window on the left side, and the roof was bright yellow. There were five cats sitting by the front door, and they were all staring at me as I walked through the front gate.

"Why was the cat afraid of the tree? Because of its

bark," I joked to my friends as we walked up to the front door. When I didn't hear George or Indie laugh, I continued with my great cat jokes. "How do cats stop crimes from happening? They call claw enforcement!"

One of the cats snarled at me, but I'm sure it was laughing at my jokes. Once I passed the cats, I knocked on the front door, but there was no answer.

"Hello?" I knocked again. "Miss Boom?"

Still, there was no answer.

"Is it open?" Indie reached forward and turned the handle. It opened. "Should we go in?"

"Miss Boom is our best chance to save the city," I said as I stepped inside the open door. "Hello? Anybody home?"

I heard a loud bang come from the end of the hallway. "Hello? Miss Boom?"

"In here," she called out. "Last door on the left in the hallway."

Cautiously, I walked forward. George and Indie followed close behind. We stepped toward the closed door, and I pushed it open.

Miss Boom stood in the middle of the room, behind a long table, filled with different gadgets and chemical formulas stored in small tubes.

Everything in the room was white. The walls were white, the ceiling was white, and the table in the middle of the room was white. The carpet was white, the chairs were white, and the cat next to the window was white.

As soon as we stepped inside the white room, there was a small explosion.

"Oh, hello, children," Miss Boom said after the smoke from the small explosion began to clear. "I was just testing how some molecular structures interact with other molecular structures. You see, a molecular structure is the three-dimensional structure of atoms inside a molecule. Once you can understand the molecular structure of a compound, it can assist in determining the reactivity, polarity, color, and magnetism of that said compound. And once you understand the molecular structure of that said compound, you can establish a deep understanding of what makes it like it is."

"Hmm, yes, yes," I said, tapping my finger on my chin and pretending to know what she was talking about. "So, you're saying that 3D movies are better than the magnetism of the polarity of matters and stuff and things and other things. Yes, yes, I agree."

Miss Boom looked at me and shook her head. "George would understand." Miss Boom patted George on the head. "Now, how can I help you?"

"Miss Boom, we need your help," Indie said. "We would love to make more invisible ink, but we've run out of lemons. There's a lemon shortage across our entire town. Nobody has any lemons. So, we were wondering if you knew how to make a substitute for lemons?"

"Interesting." Miss Boom scratched her head. "Yes, I think we can do that."

"Really?"

"But we're going to need some things. We need to create a delicate citrus balance. Get me two slices of bread, two avocados, one worm, a tub of peanut butter, a handful of sunflower seeds, and some soda."

"And that will make the formula?"

"No. That's just my lunch," Miss Boom said. Indie recoiled in disgust. "And for the formula," Miss Boom continued, "we need to activate the citric acid cycle, which is also known as the tricarboxylic acid cycle. This cycle is a sequence of chemical reactions used by aerobic organisms to release stored energy via the oxidation of acetyl-CoA. The cycle provides the foundations of certain amino acids that are used in numerous other formulas, and its importance to many biochemical pathways indicates that it was one of the earliest established components of cellular metabolism.

So, I'm going to need an orange, two glasses of water, and three tubes of the chemical compound $C_6H_8O_7$, which I have around here. You'll find all the other requirements in the kitchen, which is the first door on the left as you enter the hallway."

"Hmmm, yes, yes." I tapped my finger on my chin again, pretending to understand what she said. "You're saying that lemons would be great cyclists in a fast race with other citric acids, and it would definitely be faster than an orange. Yes, yes, I agree."

Miss Boom shook her head and turned back to her experiment. Indie, George and I all nodded to each other and then ran out of the room to the kitchen. We gathered up all the items Miss Boom had listed and then carried them back to her white science room.

Miss Boom didn't say anything as she loaded up the mixer. She put the slices of bread, two avocados, one worm, a tub of peanut butter, a handful of sunflower seeds, and soda into the mixer. She mixed them all together, mashing them up so it became a chunky liquid, and then she swallowed it in five large gulps. Once she'd finished, she wiped her mouth and turned back to the experiment and mixed the other ingredients together.

"There," she said, holding a little tube of yellow formula. "You now have a substitute for lemon juice."

"How many bottles of this can you make?"

"Only three with what I have here," Miss Boom answered. "We have more $C_6H_8O_7$ at the school so I can make more when the science room at the school opens back up, but that's all I have right now."

Only three, which equaled one spray bottle of formula each. It wasn't a lot, but it would have to do.

It was time to save the world from a Ghost Ninja attack.

CHAPTER 16

The fate of the entire living world was up to us. We had to believe in ourselves.

If we weren't brave enough, then the Ghost Ninjas would take over our town, then the country, then the world, then the galaxy, then the universe, and then the... um, well, I'm not sure if anything comes after the universe, but the Ghost Ninjas would probably conquer that as well.

George, Indie, and I sat in my bedroom talking about our plan to beat the Ghost Ninjas.

"The Ghost Ninjas said they're going to attack the police station tonight," I said. "That's where the last of the lemons are stored, and the Ghost Ninjas aren't going to stop until they've taken them. We need to ambush the remaining Ghost Ninjas at the police station. That's our best chance at stopping them."

"But we only have three bottles of the formula." George sat on the edge of my bed with his shoulders slumped forward. "What if that isn't enough? What if we fail? What if they hurt us? What if we can't protect ourselves?"

"He has a point," Indie said as she looked out the window. "It's not just about defeating the Ghost Ninjas—it's about staying alive while we do it."

I sighed as I sat down next to George on the bed and put an arm around his shoulders. "We need to try. We know the Ghost Ninjas are going to attack the police station, and this is our chance to ambush them. If we don't stop them, then who knows what will happen? I know this was all about getting a photo of the ghosts and becoming mega famous, but this has become bigger than that now. We need to stop them taking over the world. It's up to us."

Indie sat on the other side of George and rested a hand on his other shoulder. "He's right, George. We need to stop them somehow, or else they might take over our town. This place could be overrun by the Ghost Ninjas. Can you imagine how sad that would be?"

George stood up. He paced around the room while rubbing his forehead, and then turned to me and said, "I just don't know if we can stop them by ourselves. Maybe we should recruit more team members. We know that kids are the only ones who can see them, so maybe we should run a recruiting drive at school."

"There's no time," I said. "We need to do it tonight. This is our chance to surprise them."

"But I have a lot of homework to do," George continued. "And so much reading. There are a lot of books on my reading list, and it's going to take me weeks to get through them all."

"That's not a very good excuse."

"I know." George paused and then sat back down on the edge of the bed. "But I'm scared. They were some pretty nasty-looking ghosts."

"But what if we don't try and the Ghost Ninjas succeed. How would that make you feel?"

"Terrible," George agreed. He sighed again and then looked up at me. "I guess it's up to us to stop them, isn't it?"

"It is," I said. Feeling like it was the right moment to be inspirational, I clenched my fists and stood on top of my desk. I stared out the window with my most serious face and then lowered my voice. "It's go time, team. It's time to stop the crazy Ghost Ninjas."

CHAPTER 17

The police station looked different at night.

Maybe it was the shadows, or maybe it was the criminals sneaking out the window of their jail cell, but the police station definitely looked more menacing at nighttime.

The white brick building was long and narrow, with two levels of windows on either side of the front door. A single lamp hung over the door, casting a small circle of light onto the pavement in front of it. A creaking sound was resonating through the still night air. The place smelled like old socks. I'm not sure why, but I didn't have time to question it.

"What's the plan?" George whispered as we hid behind a bush.

He was dressed in a black-and-white superhero costume, looking like a cross between a ninja and a panda bear.

"We're going to ambush the Ghost Ninjas," I said. "When we see them approach the front entrance of the police station, I'm going to sneak up on them from behind and—"

"From behind?" Indie interrupted me. "You think they won't know you're coming?"

"I hope they do." I jingled my backpack. "We don't have a lot of the formula, so we need to trap the ninjas all together. I'll get their attention and lead them to you. Once we've got them together, we can use the spray to hit them all at once and take them down."

"Good plan." Indie agreed. "But—"

We were interrupted by a noise. It was a low humming noise, followed by a loud screech. The hairs stood up on the back of my neck, and a shiver ran through me. A cold chill wafted through the air.

It had to be the Ghost Ninjas.

"They're going through the back door," Indie said. "They're trying to sneak in without us seeing them."

"Then that's where we'll go!" I said. "Let's do this!"

My friends and I started running toward the back of the police station.

As we ran around the back of the police station, we spotted the ghosts approaching the rear entrance.

"Hey!" I shouted as we ran toward five ninjas. "Hey! Ghost Ninjas! Over here!"

The Ghost Ninjas turned toward us. They had their swords raised in the air. Once they saw us, they raced toward us at full speed.

As one of the Ghost Ninjas came toward us, Indie jumped into the air, pulled her legs up toward her chest like she was trying to sit on an invisible chair, and then kicked out with both feet at once—doing a sidey-spinny kicky-kick. She missed the Ghost Ninjas, but they moved back, closer together. The plan was working!

I picked up my spray bottle and ran toward the Ghost Ninjas as fast as possible. I fired five quick shots— one for each ninja!

They all fell over like puppets whose strings had been cut.

And then it was quiet again. They were gone. Just like that, they'd vanished. I looked over to George and he nodded. Indie nodded and then smiled. The first part of our plan had worked.

"Look out!" Indie said as five more Ghost Ninjas appeared out of the shadows, drifting toward the back entrance of the police station. "There's more of them!"

Indie charged forward, grabbing her spray bottle from her hip. She unleashed the spray on one of the ninjas. The Ghost Ninja tried to move out of the way, but Indie's aim was spot on! The Ghost Ninja shook for a few moments and then disappeared!

"Another one down!" Indie turned back to us. "George! Behind you!"

George turned quickly, his spray bottle ready, and then fired five squirts. He hit the ghost right in the chest and the ghost just vanished. Yes! The new formula was working perfectly!

As we came together, more Ghost Ninjas appeared.

We pressed our backs against each other and started spraying in all directions. The Ghost Ninjas were moving quickly. Some of them were dodging all our formula spray.

One Ghost Ninja swooped in and knocked George over.

"No!" I cried out, watching us lose the advantage we had gained. I stood up straight. "You Ghost Ninjas will never get away with this!"

There were other ways to get into the police station. The first was through the front door. The second was through the back door, which led directly to all the different offices within the building. And the third was through the windows, and the ghosts had a clear advantage when it came to floating through windows.

While we were distracted by fighting some of the Ghost Ninjas, the other ghosts started drifting through the windows of the police station.

We couldn't stop them from getting inside! Our plan had failed!

"We have to get inside the police station!" I shouted. "Quick!"

George, Indie, and I charged to the back door, swinging it open and running inside with our spray bottles drawn.

By the time we had gotten inside, the Ghost Ninjas had stormed past the receptionist, who let out a scream before diving under her desk in fear. She must've seen the floating swords!

"Hey!" I shouted, standing in the lobby, ready for action. "Ghost Ninjas! It's time to meet your doom!"

"You!" Sensei Smiling Warrior appeared and pointed his finger at me.

More Ghost Ninjas drifted out of the shadows. Uh-oh.

"Jake, the Ghost Ninja Destroyer," Sensei Smiling Warrior said. "It's time for you to meet your end."

CHAPTER 18

As Sensei Smiling Warrior stared at us, I could see more Ghost Ninjas appearing inside the police station. I looked around in horror and counted—one, two, three, four, five, six, seven, eight, nine, ten. Oh no! I'd run out of fingers to count them on!

The Ghost Ninjas were appearing everywhere and were taking over the police station. There were so many of them!

Indie gasped as she stood beside me. "How are there so many ghosts? Are they multiplying?"

"We're not multiplying," Sensei Smiling Warrior said. "We've heard about your formula, and we've come to collect it all. Hundreds of Ghost Ninjas from all over the world will arrive here in minutes, and we need your formula!"

That didn't sound good. Actually, it sounded quite

bad.

One of the police officers stepped out of his office and looked around.

"Hey, what's going on here? You kids can't be back here. This area is restricted," he said as he watched a sword floating through the air. "What's going on? Why is there a sword floating in my direction?"

"It's the Ghost Ninjas," I said, but the police officer was too distracted by the floating swords.

"Hey, guys," he called out to the other police officers. "You need to see this."

The police officers couldn't see the Ghost Ninjas, but they could see the swords. When one of the swords swung at the police officer, he stepped aside and tried to grab it. As he reached for it, another Ghost Ninja hit him with the handle of his sword and the officer fell to the ground. Ouch. That would've hurt.

More police officers stepped into the lobby and were grabbed by the Ghost Ninjas.

"Hey," one officer said. "What's grabbing me? What is this? What's going on?"

The police officer started swinging wildly, but it was having no effect on the ghosts. The other police officers came into the lobby and looked confused about what was happening.

As soon as they stepped out, they were attacked by the Ghost Ninjas!

As I was distracted, Sensei Smiling Warrior slapped the spray bottle out of my hand! He grabbed it and floated away!

No! The spray was our only hope of stopping them!

As I went to chase Sensei Smiling Warrior, a different Ghost Ninja swung at me. I saw his sword at the last second and rolled out of the way!

He threw a punch, but I dodged it, rolled again, and jumped up to kick him in the face. Yes!

He flew back a few feet, but he wasn't down for the count yet.

His eyes glowed red as he charged at me again. I jumped over his head and landed on top of one of the desks in the police station.

"We need to do something!" Indie yelled as she sprayed the ghosts trying to attack her. "I'm almost out of the formula!"

"I'm out!" George yelled as he dodged a different Ghost Ninja attack. "There's no more formula!"

That wasn't good. The Ghost Ninjas were winning, and my friends were out of formula!

"Hey, why are there ropes floating through the air?" A female police officer called out as a rope wrapped around her. "What's happening?"

The police struggled against the floating ropes, but it was no use. The officers were fighting back but it was clear that they weren't going to be able to last much longer against the ghosts. The Ghost Ninjas were too strong, and they wrapped the police officers into a pile with lots of heavy rope.

"What should we do?" George sounded panicked as he came up next to me.

"Watch out!" I yelled and pushed George to one side as a Ghost Ninja sword came down between us.

I rolled to my left and hid behind a desk, trying to buy some time.

I needed a new plan, but I needed time to think.

"Think, Jake," I whispered to myself as I hid behind a desk. "Think!"

"Jakey Jake..." Sensei Smiling Warrior searched for me high and low. He floated around but he couldn't find me. I stayed quiet and still as he drifted around the room sniffing for my scent. "Where did you go, Jake Spencer, the Ghost Ninja Destroyer? I need more of that formula! One bottle is not enough."

I heard a loud noise from the other end of the room—it was Indie!

She was surrounded by five other Ghost Ninjas! No!

"Stay away from her!" I shouted as I leaped to my

feet. "Let my friend go!"

"Ah, there you are," Sensei Smiling Warrior snarled. "We'll let her go if you give us all the formula. I need it all!"

Indie looked at me, and I nodded toward the door. She tossed her spray bottle in the air and then made a dash for the door. One of the Ghost Ninjas went to grab her, but I dove forward, grabbed the spray bottle and sprayed two squirts. I hit the Ghost Ninja in the arm, distracting him enough to allow Indie the chance to escape. As soon as he turned around, the Ghost Ninja had his sword pointed in my face.

"Don't move," he snarled. "And give me the rest of the formula."

"Here," I said. I handed the last of my supplies to him, defeated, knowing I had just given him even more power.

"Where's the rest of it?" the Ghost Ninja said.

"It's all we have, but we can make more of the formula if we go to the school," I said, trying not to let my voice shake. "There's a shortage at one of the ingredients, but we can make a substitute with some of the chemicals at the school."

As I said that, I looked around at the carnage.

The Ghost Ninjas had tied up all the police officers with ropes and were now holding them hostage inside their own building. The officers looked mega confused as the Ghost Ninjas floated around the police station with their swords. The Ghost Ninjas were laughing again, but I still didn't understand what was so funny.

With the police officers tied up, and with George and I captured, there was very little to stop them taking over the entire city.

The fight was over. The Ghost Ninjas had won.

CHAPTER 19

The Ghost Ninjas surrounded me.

They were floating around, snarling at me, ready to attack at a moment's notice.

George was next to my right shoulder, but I couldn't see Indie. The cops were tied up in the middle of the room, watching in disbelief as swords floated around the room. They were too shocked to fight back.

"We need to get to the school before they do," I whispered to George. "They're going to go to the science room and take all the chemicals. We need to stop them."

"But how can we beat them?" George asked. "We don't have any formula left."

"I'll cause a distraction, and then you run for the door. You need to get to the school and get the chemicals before they do."

George took a large gulp and then nodded.

"Ready," I whispered. "Go."

I jumped forward, lunging for the spray bottle near one of the tables. I knew it was empty, but it was a distraction to allow George the chance to escape.

"No!" one of the Ghost Ninjas yelled. "Stop the kid from getting the spray!"

As I grabbed the bottle, I looked over at George, who was running out the door. The distraction had worked. Awesome. I spun around with the spray bottle in my hands and started pressing the pump trigger. Nothing came out.

The Ghost Ninjas laughed, and then one said, "Silly little boy."

One of their swords raised in the air and the next thing I knew, everything went black.

I don't know how long I was knocked out for, but when I woke up, I was sitting on a chair in the police station, and my hands were tied behind my back. The police officers were tied up in the corner of the room, too afraid to move, but I couldn't see any Ghost Ninjas.

Everything was eerily quiet.

"George?" I called out. "Indie?"

There was a sharp thud at the door, which opened after the second thud. Indie rushed in with a hand-held fan.

"Jake!" she said, rushing over to me. "Where are the Ghost Ninjas?"

"I don't know," I said as Indie untied my hands. "But I think they're headed for the school to get more of the formula."

"What about George?"

"He's at the school as well," I explained. "I made a distraction while he ran out of the room. I told him to try and get there before the Ghost Ninjas."

"We have to stop them before they get to the formula ingredients," Indie agreed. "And we have to help George before they attack him."

Indie and I ran over to the police officers and untied them, but they didn't say a word. They were too shocked to speak. I tried to tell them about the Ghost

Ninjas, but their mouths just hung open, stunned that they'd witnessed floating swords and ropes.

Indie and I didn't explain it to them. We ran out the door of the police station, sprinting toward the school to save our friend.

"What's the plan?" Indie asked as she ran beside me.

"The best plan of all," I huffed. "We just need to trust ourselves."

CHAPTER 20

As Indie and I approached the school, we could hear George crying out for help from inside the far end of the main building.

"We need more formula," I said to Indie. "Miss Boom said it was stored in the science room."

"Right," Indie agreed. "We need some water, vinegar, and tubes full of the chemical compound of $C_6H_8O_7$."

"You get the formula and I'll buy some time with the Ghost Ninjas."

"How are you going to do that?"

"I don't know, but I'll figure it out."

Indie looked confused but didn't argue. She sprinted toward the science room while I ran toward the sound of George's voice. He was in the math classroom, at the back of the school.

"Get away from me!" I heard him scream. "Don't come any closer!"

I peered in the window and saw George flapping his shirt around his head as fast as he could. He was creating so much wind that the Ghost Ninjas couldn't get close enough to attack him.

I needed to help my friend.

I ran into the building, down the hallway, and grabbed a large piece of cardboard that was left outside the art room. With the large piece of cardboard under one arm, I charged into the math classroom.

"Jake!" George shouted. "Help!"

I flapped the large piece of cardboard as hard as I could, creating large gusts of wind. The Ghost Ninjas were forced back by the windy gusts! Yes! I continued to create strong wind gusts until we forced the Ghost Ninjas out the door.

"Yes!" George said as we high-fived. "Thanks, Jake!"

"Anytime," I said. "But what are you doing in the

math classroom? I thought you ran to the school to get more of the formula. It's in the science room."

"I know, but I saw the Ghost Ninjas following me, so I knew I couldn't lead them to the formula. Instead of going to the science room, I led them to the math classroom instead."

"Good plan," I agreed. "Indie is in the science room at the moment gathering supplies. We need to help her."

George agreed and we ran toward the door of the math classroom. We stopped and peered down the hallway, and when we couldn't see any more Ghost Ninjas, we sprinted to the science room. We ran inside, looking around the room until we saw Indie hiding under the teacher's desk, mixing the water, vinegar, and chemical compound of $C_6H_8O_7$ together.

"I've only managed to make one spray bottle," Indie said. "It takes time to get all the ingredients together."

"Good job," I said. "If we—"

"Finally!" A voice shouted from behind us. "We have the formula!"

Oh no!

Sensei Smiling Warrior was hovering next to us, smiling as he looked at the formula. He had found us before we had enough time to make a lot of the spray bottles!

Without thinking, I grabbed the half-empty spray bottle from Indie, commando rolled to the right, and fired a shot straight at Sensei Smiling Warrior.

He didn't move, as the spray hit him right in the face.

He stared at me in shock.

"What's happening?" he asked. "I'm fading away!"

And then he disappeared.

The other Ghost Ninjas stood behind me, completely shocked. They looked at each other, unsure of what to do next.

"Um," one of the Ghost Ninjas said, "he was our leader. We've never not had a leader before." He turned to the other Ghost Ninjas. "What do we do now?"

"You line up in a straight line," I said in my best leadership voice. "And when I ask, you step forward."

"Why would we do that?"

"Um…"

Indie stood up. "Because Jake defeated your leader, and that means Jake is your leader now."

"Oh. Clever," I said to Indie and turned back to the Ghost Ninjas. "She's right. I'm now your leader, you brainless ghosts. Now, line up."

The Ghost Ninjas nodded and then started to line up. The trick worked!

There were at least fifty Ghost Ninjas floating in the air, smiling, waiting for me to spray them.

"Yes, leader," one Ghost Ninja said. "We always do as our leader says."

I looked at Indie and George and they both nodded. My friends started making more of the formula, while I aimed the spray bottle.

"Line up," I told the Ghost Ninjas. "And then I'll give you a spray each."

The Ghost Ninjas lined up, and I sprayed each one in the face. As soon as they were sprayed, they started to disappear. Without their leader, these brainless Ghost Ninjas were so easy to trick!

Soon, all the Ghost Ninjas were gone.

Our town was safe again.

We'd saved the city, the world, and the galaxy.

"Oh no," I slapped my forehead. "I forgot to get a picture of the Ghost Ninjas!"

CHAPTER 21

After all the Ghost Ninjas had disappeared, Indie, George and I walked back to the police station. We walked in the front door and saw all the police officers sitting around eating doughnuts. They looked at us when we walked in, and Officer Hardy stood up.

"I have to admit," he said as he brushed the crumbs off his shirt, "that was a very good prank. You kids had us all believing there were ghosts around here."

"It wasn't a prank. There *were* ghosts around here," I said. "But it's all fixed now. All the ghosts have gone, thanks to this powerful formula." I placed a bottle of the spray on the desk next to Officer Hardy. "You need to store this formula and write a report that says if the Ghost Ninjas reappear in one hundred years, just use this formula to defeat them."

"Very funny," Officer Hardy laughed. "You kids sure know how to pull of an elaborate prank. That was very good."

"But—"

"Now, now." Officer Hardy shook his finger at us. "You need to know when to let a good prank go. You tricked us all with the flying swords and ropes, but you need to let it go now."

"But—"

"Now, get out of here before I arrest you for playing pranks on the police."

I looked at my friends and they shrugged. There was no use arguing with Officer Hardy.

I followed my friends out of the police station, but just as I was about to step out the door, I saw Officer Hardy take the spray bottle and write on it. I turned and looked, seeing that he had written, '*Ghost destroyer formula.*' I smiled as he placed it in his desk drawer.

As we were walking home, happy with our efforts in saving the world, George took out his phone and scrolled through social media.

"Um, guys?" he said.

Indie and I stopped and looked at him. "What is it?"

"You know how we wanted a photo of the Ghost Ninjas?"

"Did you get one?" I asked. "That would be so awesome."

"No," George shook his head. He turned the phone to face us. It was a blurry picture of something in the distance. "But someone from our school has just posted this picture on their social media account."

"Is that a zombie?" Indie asked.

"It looks like it," George said. "The person who took the photo has written a quote with it, *'When you see zombies while camping, you know it's time to leave.'*"

I turned to Indie and George and said, "I know what we're doing this weekend."

"Catching up on homework?" Indie said.

"No," I corrected her. "We're going to get a selfie with this zombie so that we'll be famous."

George laughed. "You're funny," he said. But his voice trailed off after he thought about what I'd said for a second. "Wait... what?"

"We need that photo!" I answered with confidence. "This is our chance to be super-mega-famous. All we need is a photo with that zombie..."

THE END

Also By Peter Patrick and William Thomas

Agent Time Spy Series:

Agent Time Spy 1
Agent Time Spy 2
Agent Time Spy 3
Agent Time Spy 4

*****

Middle School Super Spy:

Middle School Super Spy
Middle School Super Spy 2: Attack of
the Ninjas!
Middle School Super Spy 3: A Giant
Problem!
Middle School Super Spy 4: Space!
Middle School Super Spy 5: Evil Attack!
Middle School Super Spy 6: Daylight
Robbery!

Middle School Super Spy 7: Pirates!
Middle School Super Spy 8: Missions!

*****

Diary of a Ninja Spy:

Diary of a Ninja Spy
Diary of a Ninja Spy 2
Diary of a Ninja Spy 3
Diary of a Ninja Spy 4
Diary of a Ninja Spy 5

Made in the USA
Thornton, CO
12/03/23 02:31:19